W9-DAG-728
08/2015

Dear Parent:
Your child's love of reading starts here!

Every child learns to read in a different way and at his or her own speed. You can help your young reader improve and become more confident by encouraging his or her own interests and abilities. You can also guide your child's spiritual development by reading stories with biblical values and Bible stories, like I Can Read! books published by Zonderkidz. From books your child reads with you to the first books he or she reads alone, there are I Can Read! books for every stage of reading:

 SHARED READING
Basic language, word repetition, and whimsical illustrations, ideal for sharing with your emergent reader.

 BEGINNING READING
Short sentences, familiar words, and simple concepts for children eager to read on their own.

 READING WITH HELP
Engaging stories, longer sentences, and language play for developing readers.

 READING ALONE
Complex plots, challenging vocabulary, and high-interest topics for the independent reader.

 ADVANCED READING
Short paragraphs, chapters, and exciting themes for the perfect bridge to chapter books.

I Can Read! books have introduced children to the joy of reading since 1957. Featuring award-winning authors and illustrators and a fabulous cast of beloved characters, I Can Read! books set the standard for beginning readers.

A lifetime of discovery begins with the magical words **"I Can Read!"**

Visit www.icanread.com for information on enriching your child's reading experience.
Visit www.zonderkidz.com for more Zonderkidz I Can Read! titles.

So put on tender mercy and kindness as if they
were your clothes. Don't be proud.
Be gentle and patience.
Colossians 3:12b

To Ellie Hendren
–D.D.M.

ZONDERKIDZ

A Horse Named Bob
Copyright © 2011 by Dandi Daley Mackall
Illustrations copyright © 2011 by Claudia Wolf

Requests for information should be addressed to:
Zonderkidz, *Grand Rapids, Michigan* 49530

Library of Congress Cataloging-in-Publication Data

Mackall, Dandi Daley.
      A horse named Bob / Dandi Daley Mackall ; illustrated by Claudia Wolf.
      p. cm. — (Horse named Bob)
      Summary: Jen loves horses but her parents cannot afford to buy her one,
and so when Bob arrives next door it seems her prayers have been
answered until she realizes that neither Bob, nor his new caretaker, Mrs.
Gray, seems to want her friendship.
      ISBN: 978-0-310-71782-9 (pbk.)
      [1. Horses—Fiction. 2. Neighborliness—Fiction. 3. Christian life—Fiction. 4.
Persistence—Fiction.] I. Wolf, Claudia, ill. II. Title.
      PZ7.M1905Hnt 2011
      [E]—dc22   2009037510

Printed in China

14 15 16 /DSC/ 7 6 5 4 3

ZONDERkidz

I Can Read! 2 READING WITH HELP

A Horse Named Bob

story by Dandi Daley Mackall

pictures by Claudia Wolf

Jen loved horses.

She loved reading about horses.

She even dreamed about horses.

"Could I please get a horse?"

Jen asked her mom and dad.

"We don't have money for a horse,"

Mom said.

"Where would you keep a horse?"

Dad asked.

Then one day after school,

there was a horse!

A big, big horse was eating grass.

The horse was in Mrs. Gray's yard.

"You have a horse!" Jen cried.

Mrs. Gray frowned. She said,
"I thought it was an elephant.
My brother can't care for old Bob.
Now I have to care for him."

Jen ran home with the good news.

"I prayed for a horse," Jen said,

"and here he is! You'll see.

I'm going to be Bob's best friend."

"Here, Bob!" Jen called the horse.

But the horse did not come.

Jen held out an apple.

Bob still would not come to her.

"That horse will never come,"

said Mrs. Gray.

"He does not like anybody."

The next day, Jen tried again.

She picked grass for Bob.

"Here, Bob!" Jen called.

Bob looked up at Jen.

But he still did not come.

14

Jen sat on the fence.

"That's okay," she said.

"I'll sing you a song."

Jen sang "Jesus Loves Me."

Bob still did not come.

But Jen knew Bob was listening.

"Why are you still trying?"

Mrs. Gray asked Jen the next day.

"Bob still doesn't like anyone."

Jen felt like crying.

Maybe Mrs. Gray was right.

"Bob may not like me," Jen said,

"but I like Bob."

All week, Jen visited Bob.

She brought apples.

She sang songs.

Jen told Bob about school.

Mrs. Gray shook her head.

"Give up, little girl," Mrs. Gray said.

"That horse will never come."

"Why is Mrs. Gray so mean?"

Jen asked Dad that night.

"She's not mean, Jen," Dad said.

"I think she's lonely."

"Mrs. Gray doesn't like me there,"

Jen said. "And she's not too nice."

"Well," Dad said, "just be nice to

her anyway."

The next day Jen had a plan.

She packed two apples and a book.

"It's a horse story," she told Bob.

Then she read *Black Beauty* to him.

Bob stepped closer and closer.

Jen took out one of her apples.
"Bob doesn't want your apple,"
Mrs. Gray said.

Jen smiled at the old woman.

"This one is for you," Jen said.

Jen held out the apple.

"For me?" Mrs. Gray asked.

"I thought you'd like it," Jen said.

All of a sudden came a "CHOMP!"

Bob took a big bite of the apple.

"You came to me!" Jen said.

"Well, I'll be," Mrs. Gray said.

Bob took another bite.

The big horse let Jen pet him.

"Bob likes you!" Mrs. Gray said.

"Sorry about your apple,"
Jen said to Mrs. Gray.

She dug out the other apple.

"Here you go," Jen said.

"This is from Bob and me."

Mrs. Gray smiled.

Jen smiled too.

"Thank you, Jen," Mrs. Gray said.

Bob and Mrs. Gray ate their apples.

"I think you made a friend,"

Mrs. Gray said.

"I think I made two friends,"

Jen said.